WILDCAT WENDY AND THE PEEKABOO KID

GAZELLE BOOKS

JOY ALLEN
Boots for Charlie
Teeth for Charlie

WILLIAM MAYNE
Robin's Real Engine

JANET MCNEILL
The Snow-Clean Pinny
Umbrella Thursday

PAMELA ROGERS
All Change
The Jinx

BARBARA WILLARD
Bridesmaid
The Dragon Box

ADÈLE GERAS
Tea at Mrs Manderby's

And many other titles

Wildcat Wendy and the Peekaboo Kid

Nancy Chambers

Illustrated by James Hodgson

HAMISH HAMILTON LONDON

This story was written
with Jane Elizabeth Lockwood in mind.

First published in Great Britain 1979
by Hamish Hamilton Children's Books Ltd
Garden House, 57–59 Long Acre, London WC2E 9JZ
ISBN 0 241 10121 2

Set, printed and bound in Great Britain by
Cox & Wyman Ltd
London, Fakenham and Reading

Chapter 1

Wendy crawled out of her sleeping-bag and shook a few damp leaves from her hair. The wind was chilly, and she shivered in the cold.

Victor, her horse, was quietly

chomping some grass on the far side of the clearing.

"That's right," Wendy called out to him. "Fill yourself up. We have a hard ride ahead of us today. There won't be any time to stop for lunch or tea."

Victor nodded his head slowly up and down, and made

a whuffling sound in his nose.

Wendy ran down to the stream and dunked her face in the water—no time to bother with neck and ears. She brushed her hair, did some deep knee bends, and then made a campfire to cook her breakfast.

Soon the blaze was hot enough to boil water in a little saucepan for her coffee. While she was sipping the coffee, she popped two sausages and some left-over mashed potato into the pan. When the food got brown and crispy, she ate it straight out of the pan with her special fork with the long black handle.

"That was quite delicious," Wendy said to herself, "and very nourishing."

She looked over at Victor, who was still munching grass in his slow soft way.

"Hey," she said. "Five more minutes and we're off."

Victor nodded.

Wendy kicked a lot of dirt on top of the fire to be sure it was completely out. She packed the little pan and the long-handled fork in a saddle-bag along with the rest of her provisions.

The saddle-bag had her name on it:

Wildcat Wendy

and each of her brown leather boots was engraved with a picture of a proud fierce wildcat.

Wendy climbed into the saddle, looked around to be sure she had not left anything behind, and rode off down the trail.

Chapter 2

Wendy and Victor had been on the trail for a long time. They had already ridden over a mountain and across a desert, and now they were riding under the tall trees of the Canyon del Oro. 'Canyon del Oro' means 'Canyon of Gold' in Spanish, and Wendy wondered if there really was gold in this lonely place.

Wendy was on an important mission. In her saddle-bag she carried a message from Tiny John Tripper to the Peekaboo Kid. Tiny John had told Wendy that the message was a secret, and that she must not read it. Her job was to find the Peekaboo Kid before the next full moon and give the message to him.

"I don't know why *I* had to go on this mission," Wendy said aloud to her horse.

Victor whuffled in a sympathetic way.

"T.J. always gets *me* to do his dirty work for him," Wendy went on. "Lazy varmint."

Tiny John wasn't lazy really, and Wendy knew it. But she was getting fed up with travelling hard all day and sleeping rough at night. Complaining made her feel better.

And, to tell you the truth, Wendy was a little bit scared, too. She had never met the

Peekaboo Kid, and he sounded as though he might be very unfriendly. There were lots of places he could hide in the Canyon del Oro.

"Come on, Victor," Wendy said, giving him a nudge with the heel of her boot. "Let's be moving sharpish now. No dawdling."

Victor looked over his shoulder at Wendy, and slowly winked an eye.

"All right, Victor," Wendy said. "Perhaps a little sing-song will help you to jog along faster."

Refrain (to be hummed or whistled)

In the Canyon del Oro
we're riding along;
the sky blue above us,
and singing a song.
I'm looking for someone:
he's called Peekaboo.
And my name is Wildcat,
so how do you do.

Singing Canyon del Oro,
del Oro we sing.
There's gold all around us;
we're rich as a king.
In Canyon del Oro
the sun shines all day.
The golden light follows
us two on our way.

Wendy felt much better after singing her song, and Victor began stepping along the trail at a good smart pace.

They were both feeling quite happy with themselves, when all of a sudden they saw something that made them stop short.

In the bushes beside the trail a huge dark shape loomed out at them.

Chapter 3

Wendy tried to say something to Victor, but the only sound she made was a silly little croak.

She leaned down and touched the picture of the wildcat on her boot. That always gave her courage.

"Victor," Wendy said, after she got her voice back, "we have to see what that thing is. It hasn't moved for the last three minutes, so perhaps it isn't dangerous."

Slowly, very slowly, Wendy took her feet out of the stirrups and slid off the horse. She walked towards the bushes. Victor kept close beside her in case they had to make a quick getaway.

Finally they got near enough to see what the shape was. It wasn't a fearsome animal or a crouching giant. It was a bush

covered with a big brown blanket.

"Tarnation and bless my socks!" said Wendy. "Why ever would anyone want to do a dumb thing like that?"

Victor looked around to see if there was any good grass nearby.

Wendy walked right up to the bush. She bent down and lifted a corner of the brown blanket. It was dark underneath the bush, but she could see that there was something lying on the ground.

Wendy wanted to find out what it was. She took a deep breath, touched the wildcat on her left boot, and crawled under the blanket into the middle of the bush.

There she saw:

one white mug
two green apples
ten cheesy biscuits in a bag
one packet of marshmallows

What a puzzlement!

A funny tingle began to creep up Wendy's spine.

"Victor," she called out. "Victor, come here."

Wendy started to crawl out from the bush. But just as her head poked under the blanket:

There
right in front of her nose
were two big boots
and two long legs.

She closed her eyes tight and waited a minute, then opened them again. The boots and the legs were still there.

She was just about to shout for Victor again, when she heard a quiet voice say,

"Hello, Miss Wendy."

Chapter 4

"The name's Wildcat," Wendy said, trying to sound strong and growly. "Who are you, and why did you sneak up on me like that?"

The stranger held out his

hand to help Wendy stand up. He didn't smile at her, but he had kind eyes.

"Sorry, Wildcat," he said.

"I should think so, too," Wendy said. "Why didn't you make some noise so I would have known you were there?"

"I couldn't do my job, if I was noisy," the stranger said. "I have to stay out of sight, mostly, and just keep a watch on things."

Wendy stared hard at him. She said, "Well, I'll be horns-woggled. You must be . . . you must be the Peekaboo Kid."

The stranger looked up at the sky, then over at Victor, then down at the blanket on the bush. And then he said, very quietly,

"That's right, Wildcat."

Wendy said, "And anyway, how did you know my name in the first place?"

Peekaboo said, "It's written on your saddle-bag."

"Oh," said Wendy. "Of course."

Wendy had a lot of questions she wanted to ask the Peekaboo Kid, but first she had to complete her mission. She called Victor from his grazing, and

took the secret message from the saddle-bag.

"There," she said to Peekaboo. "It's from Tiny John. I don't know what it's about, but he said it was important."

Peekaboo read the message slowly, without saying a word. When he finished reading, he put the message in his pocket.

"Well?" said Wendy. "Aren't you going to tell me what T.J. says?"

Peekaboo didn't answer.

"Look here," Wendy said. "Tiny John trusted me to get this message to you before the next full moon, and I've done it. The full moon comes tonight. The least you can do is let me in on the secret."

The Peekaboo Kid shifted his

weight from one foot to the other. He rubbed his nose with the back of his hand. He turned his back on Wendy and looked away into the distance.

Finally he cleared his throat and said, "I reckon Tiny John doesn't want you to get hurt."

"Me? Get hurt?" Wendy said. "Hah! Fat chance!"

Peekaboo held up his hand to stop her rabbiting on. He said, "Tiny John wants you to ride straight back home. No messing."

Wendy was furious. She dived at the Peekaboo Kid and

pulled the message out of his pocket, before he could stop her. This is what it said:

"I'll be flapdoodled!" said Wendy. "So T.J. thought he could keep me out of the action. Well, he can just think again. And so can you, Peekaboo!"

Chapter 5

The Peekaboo Kid gave in and let Wendy stay. He couldn't waste time arguing with her. There was too much to do to get ready for Headlock Henry's attack.

"Is that bush with the blanket

over it supposed to be a trap?" asked Wendy.

"No," said Peekaboo. "It's a shelter for travellers. I made it."

"Oh," said Wendy. "What's your job around here anyway? I mean, what do you do all day?"

"I patrol the canyon and keep an eye on things," Peekaboo said.

"It must be lonesome sometimes," said Wendy.

"Sometimes," said Peekaboo.

"You're probably quite glad to have me for company," said Wendy.

The Peekaboo Kid started to

grin. He shook his head.

"Wildcat," he said, "we can't stand here jawing all day—"

"O.K., O.K.," Wendy said. "I'll mount up and follow you to the hide-out. And then I'll help you with the treasure. And then we'll lay a trap for Headlock Henry—"

"Hush up, Wildcat," said the Peekaboo Kid. "No more talk."

He took the blanket off the bush and wrapped the mug and food up in it. He waited until Wendy mounted Victor. Then he led them off the main trail and deeper into the forest.

The Peekaboo Kid moved as silently as an Indian. Half the time Wendy thought he had disappeared, but as soon as she had nearly given him up for lost, she'd catch a glimpse of him through the trees.

The Kid kept circling and zigzagging. He had to make sure no one was following them and that no one was lying in ambush on either side or up ahead.

"Hope he knows what he's doing," Wendy whispered in Victor's ear. "We'll never find the way back on our own."

Victor whuffled softly, as if to say, "Don't worry. We'll manage."

Much later Wendy saw the Kid signalling to her.

"Let's go, Victor," she said in her ordinary voice, which sounded very loud after being quiet for so long.

"What's up, Peekaboo?" she asked.

"The hide-out is across this stream and up behind that boulder," he said. "You wait here. I'll whistle if it's safe to come up."

Wendy and Victor waited, hardly daring to breathe.

One minute went by.

Two minutes went by.

Three minutes—and then they heard a whistle.

Wendy sat tall in the saddle, and gave Victor a nudge with her heels. The horse stepped carefully into the stream and picked his way across it.

Wendy dismounted and walked to the big boulder that covered the entrance to the hide-out.

Peekaboo showed her how to

crawl into the hide-out without bumping her head.

"Is the treasure O.K.?" Wendy said in a whisper.

"There," said Peekaboo, pointing to a square black box near the wall of the hide-out. "But it can't stay here. As soon as you're rested, we'll have to take the treasure back to town for safe-keeping."

Wendy said, "I don't need any rest, thank you very much."

She was just about to crawl back out of the hide-out when she felt something strike her arm.

"Ouch," she said, in rather a loud voice. She looked down and saw an enormous acorn on the floor of the hide-out. She picked it up and handed it to Peekaboo.

The Kid examined the acorn. "Well," he said very quietly, "it looks like we've got company."

He held the acorn so that Wendy could see what made it different from all the other acorns in the forest. There were some initials carved on one side.

"Do you know what that means?" Peekaboo said.

Wendy's heart turned over. "Yes," she whispered. "Headlock Henry."

Chapter 6

"Hey," said a nasty voice from outside, "you in there. Come out and show yourself."

The two friends in the hide-out didn't move a muscle.

"You don't have to be afraid of me, little Miss Wendy," the voice said. "Come on out. You don't want me to take away your little horsey, do you?"

Wendy signalled to Peekaboo that she would go out by herself. Headlock Henry obviously hadn't seen Peekaboo, and thought Wendy was on her own.

She crawled out of the hide-out and stood up straight, facing Headlock Henry without a flicker. He had a gang of three with him, and they had her surrounded.

"I'm not little Miss Wendy—to you or anyone else," she said. "The name's Wildcat."

"I see," said Headlock Henry with a sneer on his face. "Well, little Miss Wendy, just you step aside and let us through. We know the treasure is in there, and we aim to get it."

Wendy hoped she had given Peekaboo time to plan an unpleasant surprise for Headlock. She tried to stall him a bit longer.

"The treasure isn't in there," she said. "It's in my saddle-bag. I'll show it to you."

Headlock Henry snorted. "Don't try to kid me," he said. "I've already searched your saddle-bag. Nothing precious in there. Get out of my way, missy."

Headlock shoved Wendy aside and started to enter the hide-out. His gang were preparing to follow him, and they weren't watching Wendy. Very cautiously, stealthy as a cat, she began to edge nearer to Victor.

When she was close enough, she swung up into the saddle, pulled her special long-handled fork from the saddle-bag, and charged straight at Headlock Henry's gang.

"Take that," she yelled, poking at one of them with her weapon. "And that," as she clipped another on the shoulder.

Victor was dodging and wheeling in order to keep Wendy out of the gang's clutches. He was a brave horse and didn't care if they hit him, so long as they couldn't reach Wendy.

The battle got wilder and wilder. As they fought, Wendy noticed that they were moving nearer and nearer to the stream.

"Hi-yi, Victor," she shouted. "Let's give 'em the bath of their lives."

Victor understood exactly what Wendy meant. He reared up and gave a mighty horse-scream. The gang stood petrified, not knowing what was happening.

Victor dashed at them at full tilt and, one by one, he toppled them right into the water.

"That's far more fun than

bowling," Wendy said. "You *are* a clever horse."

Victor was breathing hard and feeling rather tired, but he gave a happy nod and a whuffle in reply.

They watched the gang spluttering and clambering out of the stream on the other side. The gang didn't even look back. They ran off into the forest as fast as their legs could carry them.

Wendy dismounted and walked back to the hide-out. She knelt down by the opening and strained her ears to hear what was going on inside.

"I can't hear a thing," she said finally. "You don't suppose they've knocked each other out, do you?"

Victor shook his head and went back to his grazing.

"Stone the crows," Wendy said to herself. "I can't sit here like a wet noodle. Better go inside and see whether it's good news or bad news."

The sight that met her eyes

made her roar with laughter. She laughed and laughed until the tears came.

"Why," she gasped, "why, if it isn't little Miss Henry!"

Wendy exploded into whoops of laughter again, because there was Henry—big, tough Headlock Henry—neatly rolled up in the brown blanket and tied with rope all round. But what really tickled Wendy most was the sight of Headlock's head.

For there, stuck firmly between his open jaws, was one of the juicy green apples.

Chapter 7

"It was the only way to keep him quiet while I went out to make sure the rest of the gang had vamoosed," the Peekaboo Kid said later to Wendy.

They were sitting by a blazing

campfire, sharing the other apple, the cheesy biscuits, and some clear cold stream water out of the mug.

"Well, I'm glad H.H. promised not to yowl any more," Wendy said. "I know he's a bully, but I'd hate to leave him with an apple stuck in his mouth all the way back to town."

Peekaboo nodded.

"Are we going to stay here tonight?" Wendy asked. "I'd better get Victor settled, if we are."

"I reckon we should get back to town kind of quickish,"

Peekaboo said. "Tiny John will be worried about us. We can set off as soon as the full moon rises. I'll be able to see well enough then."

"O.K.," Wendy said. "We don't dare untie little Miss Henry, so we'd better strap him on Victor's back for the journey. Right? And I'll walk with you."

"Wildcat," said Peekaboo, "why do you call him little Miss Henry?"

Wendy scowled and said, "No one calls *me* little Miss Wendy more than once and gets away with it."

"I see," said Peekaboo, and changed the subject. "Let's have a marshmallow."

Wendy stuck a marshmallow on the prongs of her long-handled fork and held it over the fire. When the marshmallow was nicely burnt on the outside and sweet and runny on the inside, she gave it to Peekaboo.

"Yum," he said. "That was delicious."

"And very nourishing," said

Wendy. "And there are twenty-three more marsh-mallows still to eat."

"That's just dandy," said the Peekaboo Kid, and he settled down to wait for the rise of the full moon.

In the Canyon del Oro
we're walking along.
The moon high above us,
and singing a song.
We've caught Headlock Henry;
I've met Peekaboo.
And my name is Wildcat,
so how do you do.

Singing Canyon del Oro,
del Oro we sing.
There's gold all around us;
we're rich as a king.
In Canyon del Oro
the moonshine is bright.
Its silver glow follows us
all through the night.